MEET TEAM PRIME

A Bantam Book 978 0 857 51153 9

Published in Great Britain by Bantam, an imprint of Random House Children's Books
A Random House Group Company.

This edition published 2012

1 3 5 7 9 10 8 6 4 2

HASBRO and its logo, TRANSFORMERS PRIME and all related characters are
trademarks of Hasbro and are used with permission.
Copyright © 2012 Hasbro

The Random House Group Limited supports the Forest Stewardship Council (FSC®), the leading international
forest certification organization. Our books carrying the FSC label are printed on FSC®-certified paper.
FSC is the only forest certification scheme endorsed by the leading environmental organizations, including
Greenpeace. Our paper procurement policy can be found at www.randomhouse.co.uk/environment

MIX
Paper from
responsible sources
FSC® C009967

MEET TEAM PRIME

BANTAM BOOKS

Attention, Transformers fans!

Look out for these items when you read

this book. Can you spot them all?

HOLOGRAM

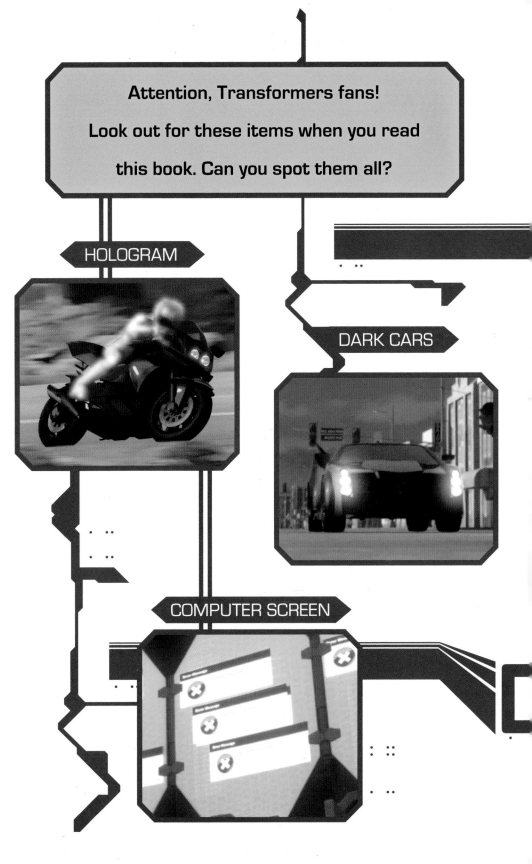

DARK CARS

COMPUTER SCREEN

Optimus Prime and his Autobot team
live on Earth.

They patrol the planet to defend it
against the evil Decepticons.

Optimus Prime is the leader of the team. "We must protect humankind," he tells his friends.

Optimus can change into a Big Rig truck to blend in on Earth.

Another member of the team is Arcee. She cruises the streets as a motorbike and projects a hologram of a rider so that no one suspects anything.

The Autobots' number one rule is to keep a low profile.

While on patrol, Arcee is followed. She stops at a restaurant to hide in the car park.

A boy named Jack sees Arcee and thinks she is a normal motorbike.

Jack gets on to pretend for a moment that he owns such a cool motorbike.

Two dark cars slowly pull up. They are Decepticons.

The cars rev their engines and roar towards Arcee.

"Oh, no!" yells Arcee. She takes off down the street, with Jack still on board.

The Decepticons race after them.

"Whoa!" Jack cries in surprise.

"Do not let go!" orders Arcee.

"Who said that?" asks Jack. He had never heard of a talking motorbike.

A yellow-and-black car drives up and honks. It is the Autobot named Bumblebee. He lost his voice in a battle long ago and now communicates without speaking.

"Is that a friend of yours?" asks Jack.

"Family," answers Arcee.

The dark cars are gaining on them.

Arcee jumps over a bridge and screeches

to a stop . . . right in front of a boy called Raf!

Raf is playing with a remote-control car.

Arcee and Bumblebee quickly change form. They turn to fight the Decepticons, who have changed from cars into robots.

Jack and Raf run down the street to safety.

"What are they?" Raf asks.

"Talking cars that turn into robots – or maybe the other way around," Jack answers.

Bumblebee and Arcee beat back the Cons.

Arcee reports over the radio.
"Arcee to Optimus!" she says.
"The Cons are back! They
would be scrap metal by now, but two
humans got in the way."

"Humans?" cries Optimus Prime. "If our
enemies saw them with you, the humans
will be in great danger. You must bring
them here."

Arcee and Bumblebee head out to
look for Raf and Jack. They find the
boys walking together.

Bumblebee drives up to Raf and
honks his horn. The car door pops open.

"He wants me to get in," says Raf.

"Just you? How do you know?" asks Jack.

Raf understands Bumblebee. "Your lift is over there," he says.

Arcee is nearby in motorbike form.
Someone else sees Arcee, too. A girl
called Miko watches them. She sees
Arcee change into a robot.

Arcee speaks to Jack. "Come with me," she says. "It is for your safety."

"Dude, go with her!" shouts Miko.

Arcee sees the girl. Now that Miko
has seen an Autobot, she has to keep
the secret, too.

"Oh, scrap," says Arcee. "Come on." She tells Miko to come with them.

"Woo-hoo!" yells Miko. She cannot wait to ride such a cool bike.

The Autobots have a secret base in the middle of the Nevada desert.

Ratchet is the Autobot who operates the GroundBridge transport system, which allows the Autobots to go anywhere on the planet in just moments.

When Arcee and Bumblebee return to the base, Ratchet, Bulkhead and Optimus are surprised to see three humans with them.

Miko marches right up to Bulkhead.
He is a huge Autobot who is very strong
and can turn into an off-road vehicle.

"I am Miko. What are you? Are you a
car? I bet you are a truck."

"We are autonomous robotic organisms from the planet Cybertron," says Optimus. "We are here to protect Earth from Decepticons."

"Why are they here?" asks Jack.

"Our home planet was destroyed," Optimus explains. "The Decepticons wish to take over Earth. It is best that you remain under our watch for now."

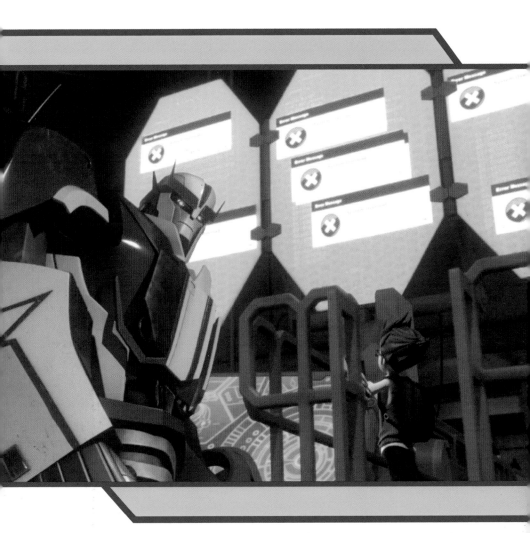

"They have no protective shells!" Ratchet, the medic Bot, grumbles.

His computer screen shows an error message.

"I think I can fix that," says Raf.

Ratchet is amazed to see Raf quickly fix the computer.

"These humans are now part of Team Prime," says Optimus Prime. "And Team Prime is a family."

"Awesome!" yells Miko.

Jack, Raf and Miko cannot wait to see what adventures lie ahead!